You, Me and Thing:

You, me and Thing

The Mummy That Went Moo

You, me and Thing

Karen McCombie

Illustrated by Alex T. Smith

faber and faber

First published in 2013
by Faber and Faber Limited
Bloomsbury House,
74–77 Great Russell Street,
London, WC1B 3DA

Typeset by Faber and Faber
Printed in England by CPI Group (UK) Ltd, Croydon, CR0 4YY

A CIP record for this book
is available from the British Library

ISBN 978–0–571–27263–1

FSC
www.fsc.org
MIX
Paper from
responsible sources
FSC® C101712

2 4 6 8 10 9 7 5 3 1

Contents

A little (old) Thing

Can I ask you a question?

(Warning: you're going to think it's a very stupid one.)

Do you know how old you are?

You might be shouting, 'Of course I do!'

Or 'Are you *mad*?!'

Well, I'm not mad.

I'm Ruby Morgan and I'm ten years old.

And here's another fact – I have two best friends. One is called Jackson Miller and he is ten, same as me.

The other is Thing and it doesn't have a *clue* how old it is.

So maybe my question wasn't so stupid *after* all!

Now maybe *you* have a question for *me*, like 'How did you end up being friends with a thing called Thing?'

Or 'What *is* Thing?'

Or just plain '*Huh?*'

OK, if you want to know about Thing, then I have to start with Jackson. (Sorry, but that's how it is.)

You know, I didn't like Jackson one bit when we first met.

Which was tricky because he'd moved in right next door.

(Oh *boy*, did I hate spotting him dancing round his bedroom in his boxer shorts and socks. Bleurgh!)

Then everything changed.

One day, me and the most annoying boy I'd ever met (yep, Jackson) made a strange discovery. There, nuzzled and nervy in the trees behind our gardens, was a small, shy Thing.

It had gingery fur, stumpy wings and – get this – it could *talk*.

So that's what we knew about Thing, pretty much straight away.

But there was a bunch of stuff we *didn't* know.

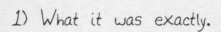

TOP 5 THINGS ME & JACKSON DIDN'T KNOW ABOUT THING

1) What it was exactly.

2) Whether it was a boy or a girl.

3) Why it could talk and do magic. (Yep, you heard that right!!)

4) Why it had wings but couldn't fly.

5) How old it was.

Now, about number five on the list ... We **DID** try to find out, not so long ago.

'Hey, are you a *kid*? Or ancient, like Ruby's cat?' Jackson asked it.

'Not *know*, thank you,' Thing answered in its funny, purry voice.

Then it had wobbled from side to side and let out a tiny burp. (Well, Jackson **HAD** just fed it eleven jelly babies in a row.)

And that, it seemed, was the end of *that*.

Till our school trip to the museum. When me and Jackson found out that Thing might be really, **REALLY** old.

HOW old exactly?

Well, maybe older than the ivy-covered cottage I live in.

Perhaps even older than the gnarly thick oak trees that used to squat in Muir Wood (before they all got chopped down).

Yes, older than your *nan*, even . . .

So settle down, relax and let me tell you a tale about museums and mummies, magic and mooing, and mayhem in the men's loos.

PS One thing me and Jackson DO know for sure; life with our little old Thing is never, EVER dull . . .

DRIP, DOINK!

Every school day, as soon as we get home,
me and Jackson run into our separate-but-
next-door-houses and do *this* . . .

FLING!

(The sound of schoolbags being hurled off.)

SWITCH!

(School uniform getting swapped for
comfy stuff.)

LIE!

(That's us telling our parents we're off to
hang out, just the two of us.)

ZOOM!

(That's me and Jackson rushing down to the bottom of our gardens to hang out with Thing.)

But one particular Monday, I was struggling to **ZOOM.**

'You have *got* to be kidding, Ruby!' Mum laughed, watching me pull on a too-tight cagoule (age 6) and wobble my way into Dad's giant wellies.

'What?' I said with a shrug.

'*Surely* you and Jackson aren't planning on meeting at the trees today!'

'Why not?' I replied. 'It's just a bit damp!'

We both stared out of the kitchen window at the torrential rain.

'Maybe it's not as bad as it looks,' I mumbled, knowing it was probably *worse* than it looked.

It had been raining since breakfast and the back garden was quite possibly a mud lagoon by now.

'Why don't you and Jackson stay *here*, indoors, instead?' Mum suggested, picking up a brand-new packet of Jaffa Cakes and wiggling it at me temptingly.

'Nah, I'm all right,' I lied, beginning to drool. 'I'll just have a couple of mushrooms instead.'

As I went to open the fridge door, I could feel Mum staring at me.

But I had to bluff it out; Thing – whose diet consisted of mushrooms, mushrooms, mushrooms and jelly babies – might be hungry.

'Raw vegetables are *very* good for you,' I chattered, avoiding Mum's what-is-she-on-about? gaze. 'We've been learning that at school. Bye!'

I headed quickly out of the back door, my rubbery feet flip-flapping, clenched fists mushing up the mushrooms and cheeks pink from fibbing . . .

SQUELCH, *SLURP*, SQUELCH, *SLURP* went my boots on the slippy-slidey lawn.

DRIP, *DOINK*, DRIP, *DOINK* went the

rain from the edge of my blue plastic hood on to the tip of my nose.

'Thing?' I hissed, throwing my leg over the low stone wall.

There was no sign of Jackson. He hadn't chickened out, just cause of a tiddly bit of a monsoon, had he?

'Peh . . .' I heard in reply.

I peeked down at Thing's den, which happened to be an old Scooby-Doo Mystery Machine van parked in some roots and camouflaged with ferns, twiglets and scuttling bugs.

And there it was, flopped out flat on its tummy inside. It looked like a tiger-skin rug from the olden days, when people thought it was cool to kill things and turn them into carpets.

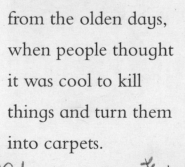

'Are you all right?' I asked, worried that it might have caught a chill.

What a dumb thing to say. Thing was a wild(ish) animal, after all. It was able to adapt to all weathers and not have to worry about wearing a vest and always carrying a tissue.

'Is all right, Rubby,' mumbled Thing, forcing itself up to a sitting position, its legs now dangling out the open back doors of the Mystery Machine. 'I just feeling . . . What is human-ing wordie for *this*?'

It sank down into itself, as if all its bones were dissolving, as if it was deflating like a furry balloon.

'Hey, cool trick!' roared Jackson, all of a sudden scrabbling down from the top of his garden's high fence.

He had a big, rainbow-coloured golf umbrella hoisted over his head.

'It's not a *trick*,' I said, rolling my eyes at Jackson. 'Thing's trying to describe how it feels!'

'Ah – OK!' grinned Jackson, as if it was the start of a game of charades. 'Hmm . . .'

He rubbed his chin thoughtfully, staring at our sunken squirrelly/fairy/troll-ish friend.

'Heavy?'

'Peh!' grumbled Thing, rolling its own bushbaby eyes.

'Embarrassed?' Jackson tried again. 'Hollow? Itchy?'

Wow, I had learned something new about Jackson – never have him on my team for charades. He was useless.

'Thing's *bored*, Jackson!' I jumped in. '*That's* what it's trying to tell us!'

'Yeah? Well, maybe this will help!' he answered, crouching down and pulling a packet of jelly babies from his pocket.

'Ooh, yes, please!' said Thing, immediately brightening up, and snouting in the air for a whiff of fruity sugariness.

'But how come you're bored?' asked Jackson, struggling to open the packet *and* hold on to his heavy umbrella. 'Aren't you *used* to rain, Thing? Before you got here, you lived in a forest all your life!'

Once upon a not-very-long-ago time, the endless Muir Wood backed right on to my garden. Now the endless Forest View Housing Estate backs on to it instead. (No guesses which one was prettier.)

'Yes, **please**, but this rain too **wet**,' Thing replied, rocking impatiently from side to side, as it eyed up the sweets. 'Old forest rain nice. Nice **thin** rain.'

'*Thin* rain?' Jackson mumbled, and he tried to tear the stubborn jelly-baby packet open with his teeth. 'I didn't know the weather came in different sizes!'

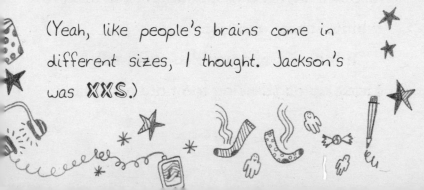

(Yeah, like people's brains come in different sizes, I thought. Jackson's was XXS.)

'Oh, yes, please!' Thing nodded, its eyes locked on the bag Jackson was wrestling with. 'Thin rain is because of big trees. Big trees look like *that*.'

Thing pointed at what Jackson was holding.

'The trees were like *jelly babies*?!' Jackson asked, deeply confused.

'*No!*' I sighed. 'In your *other* hand! Thing's pointing at your *umbrella*! When it lived in the forest, the thick canopy of the trees will have shielded the forest floor from a lot of the rain!'

Jackson blinked at me stupidly, like he had brain-freeze.

It was that same expression he got on his face when Miss Wilson, our teacher, tried to explain where apostrophes go.

'Whatever!' he mumbled eventually, giving up on thinking too hard and finally

yanking the sweet packet open instead. 'Help
yourself!'

'Mmmm,' Thing purred happily, delicately
taking a red jelly baby and biting its head
off.

Well, Jackson *might* be a complete donut,
but hurray for him cheering Thing up.

I hated the idea of Thing being bored and
lonely more than anything.

Actually, that's not true; what I dreaded MOST was Thing being discovered by someone who wasn't *us*. Someone who might flip out at the sight of a tiny, talking creature and run off and tell the world. What would happen to Thing then?

Brrrr, I hated to even think about it.

Which is why it *had* to stay hidden and happy in this little leftover straggle of trees and shrubs.

NO ONE but me and Jackson could ever, *ever* know about it . . .

'Can new friend have jelly baby, please and *thank* you?' Thing suddenly purred.

AARGHH!!

I shot a scared look at Jackson and saw it ping-ponged right back at me.

'*What* new friend?' Jackson asked tensely, his eyebrows meeting in one long, blond caterpillar of concern.

Had some kid from the estate come exploring here? Maybe they'd kicked their ball into the bushes, or come after a bounding, snuffling dog, or . . . or . . .

I couldn't think straight – my head was melting with panic.

Whoever had found Thing, and *however* they'd found it, all I knew for sure was that it meant **TROUBLE**.

With a capital **EVERYTHING!**

Oh, hold on. Maybe me and Jackson had panicked a little bit too soon.

'*Here* my friend!' said Thing, gazing up at

us with its saucer-round eyes and pointing a fuzzy finger at . . . an empty space by its side!

I felt my whole body sag with relief, like a dunked teabag.

So Thing hadn't been discovered by some kid from Willow Avenue, or one of the other roads on the new estate.

Which meant there was no chance of the police, or army, or government scientists coming to catch it with big nasty nets.

'Ha!' Jackson laughed. 'You mean you have an invisible friend?'

'What *is* nin-zivvable, please?' asked Thing.

'It means you can't see it,' I tried to explain. Thing could speak a whole bunch of languages – from starling to toad – but it wasn't exactly fluent in human quite yet.

'But *I* see it, Rubby!' Thing replied indignantly. 'It *there*! See?'

Me and Jackson leaned in closer, still clutching our random umbrellas and mushrooms and jelly babies.

Oh.

On the blue plastic floor of the van was a teeny, weeny bug. It had – let's see – one . . . two . . . three . . . *lots* of legs, which were doing the insect version of a Mexican wave.

'Is woodlouse,' Thing explained.

'Oh! Is it one of your friends from the forest?' I asked, suddenly remembering

that Thing had once told us about some woodlice he'd been buddies with.

'No . . . They is deaded long, long, long time ago. Long, long, long long, *long* time ago,' said Thing, taking the yellow jelly baby Jackson was holding out and placing it beside the bug. The bug scuttled straight on top of it.

'But *how* long a long time ago?' I asked, wondering if we might be able to work out just how old Thing was at last.

'Not *know*, thank you,' said Thing, with a furry shrug. 'They all deaded when frosty came instead of sunny.'

Frosty . . . instead of sunny?!

I didn't realise at the time, but Thing had just given us the first EVER clue about its age.

I didn't realise it because I was too busy hurting.

'Oooooowwww!' I yelped, slapping a hand to my face.

'What? What's happened?' asked a worried Jackson.

His brain really *was* extra, extra small.

He hadn't even noticed that he'd stuck an umbrella spoke *right* in my eye . . .

Very funny
(I don't think)

Twenty minutes later, and I was in a warm, dry room.

In pain.

Waiting to be seen by a doctor.

'Didn't I say that you should have both stayed indoors with a packet of biscuits?' Mum gently teased me. 'None of this would've happened if you'd been sitting in your room with a Jaffa Cake!'

Very funny (I don't think).

It was hard to laugh – even a little bit – when my eyeball felt like it was on fire.

But hey, everyone thought they were jokers today.

Even the nurse who'd seen me when we arrived at hospital.

Once she'd checked that my left eyeball was still there (and only scratched, she said) she'd checked out my feet.

'Catch a lot of rain in those, do you?' she asked, nodding down at Dad's flapping great wellies and my little stick legs.

Now it was the doctor's turn.

'Hello, there! I'm Dr Narindra!' a man with a stethoscope announced, throwing the cubicle curtain open theatrically. 'So, young lady, I hear you picked a fight with an umbrella, and lost!'

I didn't try to answer him, cause I was

afraid all that would come out of my mouth
would be a low groan.

'And is this the offending weapon?' he
asked, turning to look at Jackson.

Jackson was perched at the end of the bed,
holding his stupid umbrella across his chest
like a soldier's rifle.

'Uh, yeah,' he mumbled.

Actually, Jackson was the only person who *hadn't* made fun of me. Guilt and worry had turned him quiet as a woodlouse.

'Planning on going for her *other* eye?' the doctor said to him, with a wry smile. 'Otherwise, you could put your umbrella down, you know!'

'Uh, no . . . it's OK, I'll hang on to it,' Jackson answered, gripping the slightly unfurled umbrella.

I don't know why he'd brought it with him to the hospital in the first place. But I guess it *was* all a mad rush after the eye-poking incident.

I hadn't even realised he was in the car on the way to Accident & Emergency till Mum turned to him in the back seat and asked him to stop playing with the switch that made the windows go up and down.

'Please yourself!' the doctor said breezily,

before taking something out of his pocket.
'Now, then, young lady. Can you look up?
I'm just going to put these anaesthetic drops
in your eye ...'

EEK!
OUCH!
OOOOOOOO . . .

'Open and shut your eyes a few times,' the
doctor was saying, 'and it'll get better, Ruby,
I promise!'

BLINK!

(It was like looking up at the world from
the bottom of a swimming pool.)

BLINK!

(Bit clearer – but everything was double, with twin whirls of rainbows around them.)

BLINK!

(How funny! Standing behind the doctor, it looked like Jackson had *two* heads. His normal one, and a smaller one, just about chest height.)

EEK!

That was no optical illusion! A small gingery hand had just popped up from behind the umbrella and WAVED at me.

What was *Thing* doing here?!

'Ah, well done, Ruby! No need to tell *you* to keep your eyes wide open!' said the doctor, as he shone a blinding light into my eye.

The beam of light was so strong it felt like

it was right inside my head.

(The doctor could probably see the word 'Eek!' floating around inside.)

'Uh-huh ... mmm-hmmm ...' muttered the doctor, moving his light and himself about.

For a second, my good eye got a clear view of Jackson over Dr Narindra's shoulder.

I scowled at him as best I could.

He shrugged back at me.

Then I saw him glance worriedly down – at a pair of ears poking up from behind the umbrella ...

'Hide Thing!!' I felt like yelling. 'Quick, before Mum or the doctor turn around and spot it!'

He might have noodles for brains, but at least Jackson seemed to receive my psychic message.

He let go of one end of the umbrella and pushed Thing's head down, out of sight.

'Right, I'll just ask the nurse to come back in and put a patch on that . . .'

I didn't listen to the rest of what Dr Narindra was saying. Mum did, though, and followed him out of the cubicle for a chat.

Which gave Jackson and me the chance for a whispery chat of our own.

'Why did you bring Thing here?' I hissed.

'I *had* to!' Jackson whispered back. 'It was worried about you!'

'There there, Rubby!' purred Thing, popping up from behind the umbrella and reaching out for a hug.

I didn't dare lift it up to me, in case someone swooped back through the cubicle curtain. Instead, I took hold of its tiny paws.

'Thing was all panicky and . . . and AARGHH,' Jackson muttered in my ear. 'I was worried what it might do, if I just left it there in the trees!'

OK, I could
suddenly see his point.

Whenever Thing feels cross, or
stressed, or just plain AARGHH, it has
a bad habit of doing, er, bad magic.

When I say bad, I don't mean *evil*, I
just mean *rubbish*.

Rubbish magic that normally gets us
into terrible muddles and messes ...

If Jackson had left a panicky Thing
behind in the trees, it might have set off
a spell, turning the tree branches into
golf umbrellas or the leaves into jelly
babies or something.

And what would the
neighbours in Willow Avenue

have made of that, if they'd happened to be putting out their recycling?

'Rubby?' Thing suddenly asked.

'Yes, Thing?' I looked down at it.

'You still got *eye*?'

'Yes, I've still got my eye,' I smiled down at Thing, as I squeezed its paws tight.

SWOOOSH!

'Aw! Isn't that lovely! Having a little cuddle, are we?' boomed the nurse, ripping back the curtain, exposing us to Mum, Dr Narindra and anyone else who might fancy a nosey.

NOOOO!

I wasn't worried about Thing being spotted; at the first SW- *of* SWOOSH, it had dipped out of sight behind the unfurled umbrella.

I was worried that the nurse and everyone else might think — horror of horrors — that

I'd been hugging *Jackson*.

And what if they thought that *Jackson* (shiver) was my *boyfriend*!

'I, uh, have to go to the, uh, loo . . .' mumbled Jackson, as pinkly cheeked as me.

Holding his umbrella rifle across his chest, he scrambled to his feet and hurried off towards the door.

'Now let's get some protective gauze on you,' muttered the nurse.

As she taped a white patch across my bad eye, my good eye caught a glimpse of a pair of red, furry ears and two huge eyes peeking over Jackson's shoulder.

Thing was waving . . . no, it was blowing me a kiss!

How cute was that?

Cute, and highly *dangerous*.

I bit my lip and hoped my non-boyfriend got Thing out of sight, super-quick . . .

Miss Wilson's witherings

'Ruby?' our teacher called out, as she took the register.

'Here, Miss Wilson!' I answered, just like I usually did.

'Ruby! What's wrong?' gasped Miss Wilson, glancing over at me and realising I didn't exactly *look* like I usually did.

I mean, I don't usually come to school disguised as a pirate.

All I needed was a parrot on my shoulder, to match the white patch of padding taped across my eye …

(Yeah, I know pirate patches are normally black, but hey, I'm a GOOD pirate!)

'I have a scratch on my cornea,' I told her, aware that EVERYONE was staring at me as if I had a head made of cheese.

'Oh, dear!' Miss Wilson sympathised. 'How did that happen?'

'She stuck her eye in my umbrella!' Jackson joked.

The whole class laughed.

Miss Wilson didn't. She gave Jackson one of her withering looks.

(Her withering looks can shrink you just as easily as one of those 'Drink Me' bottles in *Alice in Wonderland*.)

Jackson didn't notice, he just grinned at the rest of our giggling classmates.

He'd felt bad yesterday, when we were at the hospital. But once Mum had driven us home and he'd sneaked Thing safely back to the trees, he'd relaxed, and turned back into the big baboon I knew so well.

'But seriously, how did you get hurt, *RUBY*?' she asked, stressing my name loudly, so Jackson knew she didn't want to hear any more of his nonsense.

I hesitated for a second.

Well, you would, if you were trying to work out what to tell your teacher.

I mean, the truth would sound like a squashy fat lie, wouldn't it?

'I was bending down to see our pet Thing's nin-zivvable friend, when Jackson's umbrella spoke poked me in the eye.'

Quick as a flash, I deleted the first part of that sentence, and said simply, 'Jackson's umbrella spoke poked me in the eye.'

'Well!' Miss Wilson tutted. 'I suppose that's a lesson for us all – umbrellas can be dangerous as well as useful in this weather!'

Thirty pairs of eyes – well, twenty-nine and a half – turned to stare at the rain splattering down outside our class for the second day running.

'I hope it's not like this on Friday . . .' Miss Wilson muttered.

Friday was the day for our school trip. We were going to the museum in the next town.

'And while I'm thinking about our class

outing, can anyone tell me what they're most looking forward to seeing?'

Miss Wilson looked hopefully around the class, and a few arms shot up.

'The cafe!' Jackson called out, even though she wasn't pointing at him.

Everybody laughed. Except for Miss Wilson, of course.

'Jackson,' she sighed, giving him *another* withering look, 'if you can't say something sensible, I'd prefer it if you said nothing at all.'

Nice try.

But expecting Jackson not to act or speak like a big donut is a bit like expecting my old cat Christine to stay awake for more than ten minutes at a time.

'Anyone, else?'

Miss Wilson glanced around and nodded at Jada.

'The Egyptian section, Miss Wilson!'

'What, with *real* dead mummies?!' yelped Jackson.

'Yes, there *is* a display of ancient Egyptian relics, Jackson,' she answered him calmly. 'But they are only copies of originals from the British Museum.'

'Awesome! A *real* dead mummy! Woooo . . . !' Jackson yelped, holding his arms out in front of him and imitating the sort of bandaged spook you'd see in *Scooby-Doo*.

'Quiet, Jackson! Anyone *else*?' Miss Wilson

shouted out sternly, over the top of the sniggering.

Ali stuck his hand in the air.

'Please, Miss Wilson!' he said excitedly. 'I wanna see the bit with the Vikings!'

All the boys in the class made various 'yesss!!' type noises.

We did a project about the Vikings last term (before Jackson came to our school).

The boys really, **REALLY** liked that project. Not for the interesting facts like Vikings leaving milk out for elves, or how the goddess Freya cried golden tears.

Oh, no. They went crazy for the gory stuff. Here were some of their favourite facts:

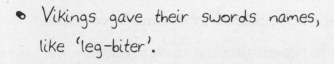

- Vikings gave their swords names, like 'leg-biter'.

- They'd set fire to buildings with their enemies locked inside.

- The god Odin yanked out one of his eyes so he could drink in some magic fountain.

Remembering that last one made me wince.

'Oh – is it hurting, Ruby?' Miss Wilson asked, noticing that I'd slapped my hand over my padded eye patch.

'No, it's just—'

'Have they got any of those brilliant Viking helmets? With the big cow horns on them?!' Jackson burst in.

'Jackson!' snapped Miss Wilson. 'Can I remind you that Vikings *didn't* have helmets with horns on them; it's just a myth.'

'But I've seen them in cartoons! They're *so* cool! Get *this*: they could headbutt their enemies and ram the pointy bits in their eyes!'

For the second time in under a minute, I winced.

'Jackson – that's ENOUGH!'

At the sharp snap of her voice, Jackson shut up.

(It wouldn't last.)

'Now, of course we'll look around *all* the exhibits at the museum,' Miss Wilson carried on. 'But the main reason we're going is to see a new show; a history of Muir Wood. Which

is particularly interesting now that
our local forest is gone.'

Ooh!

In the excitement of nearly losing
an eye (sort of), I'd forgotten about
that. My little old cottage sat at
the edge of the woods for a couple
of centuries. Lots of girls like me

had probably grown up there and scrabbled around in the trees, exploring, making dens and pretending to look for fairies.

I was the last of those girls, and I missed the woods madly.

Not as much as Thing, of course.

Hey, that gave me an idea . . .

Maybe the exhibition would give me and Jackson some clues about Thing's old life!

'Excuse me, Miss Wilson?'

At the sound of Jackson's voice, I turned to look at him.

(Then turned a bit more, when I realised I couldn't see out of my left eye.)

'*Yes*, Jackson?' said Miss Wilson, sounding less irritated with him now that he'd put his hand up nicely.

'About the trip . . .'

Ah, was he thinking

what *I* was thinking? Was he going to ask
more about the Muir Wood exhibit?

'Yes, Jackson?'

'*After* we've seen the real dead mummy
and the cool Viking horned helmets and the
stuff about the trees . . . *then* do we get to go
to the cafe?'

You know, Thing's mini-friend the
woodlouse probably had more brains than
Jackson Miller.

Actually, stop right there.

Stick your pinkie out. That's a pretty small
fingernail on there, right?

And a woodlouse is only about half its size
(i.e. titchy).

Who would've expected that something
so small could lead to something so big, bad
and mad happening?

Not me.

Not Jackson.

Probably not you.

But it did, as you'll see just a *teeny* bit further on in my story . . .

The opposite of normal

Dad said two things when I got home.

The first was: 'Yo ho ho!'

(I'd had pirate jokes ALL day at school. Grrr.)

The second was: 'I don't think you should play outside with Jackson – you need to stay indoors and rest that eye.'

So I stayed indoors, but it wasn't very restful. With only one eye working, everything seemed slightly not-quite-where-it-should-be, and I kept tripping over stuff.

(Try closing one of your eyes for five minutes and walking around your house. Count the bruises on your shins later.)

After bumping around a bit, I decided it might be safest to lie on my comfy bed with

Christine cat and read a book.

This was OK for a while, but I kept being distracted by my nose.

(Two eyes open: it's practically invisible. One eye open: there it is . . . a big, looming nose. *Weird*.)

To distract me from my distracting nose, I leaned forward and stroked Christine, hoping she might wake up and purr at me. But she was more interested in playing dead, so I got up and wandered over to my bedroom window, to watch how rainy the unstoppable rain was.

Not so very long ago, my view would've been of tweeting birds sheltering in the branches of the large oak tree that grew at the side of my house.

But now – in place of the tree and the birds – there was Jackson's house, and Jackson's bedroom window in particular.

I didn't expect to see him in his room, of course. Right about now he'd be in the trees, chatting to Thing, huddled underneath his deadly umbrella.

Or perhaps *not* ...

Cos there was Jackson, pogoing around his room to music I couldn't hear.

I opened my window, shouting and waving across, hoping to catch his attention.

I got a wave back, but not from Jackson . . .

Thing, perched on Jackson's shoulder, had seen me.

Huh? What was it doing in Jackson's room??? (Apart from dancing and waving, I mean.)

And by the worried look on Thing's face, it looked more like a 'help!' rather than a 'hello' sort of a wave.

'Jackson!'

'JACKSON!'

'*JACKSON!!*' I called out.

It was no use. Above the *boom-boom* of the music he couldn't hear me, and I couldn't rescue Thing.

'Dad!' I said ten seconds and a downward set of stairs later. 'My eye is completely rested now please can I go next door and

ask Jackson something about our homework
thanks *bye*!'

'Um, OK . . . !' I faintly heard Dad's
voice as I hurtled out of our cottage down
our winding path and round to the stone
driveway of Jackson's house.

Ten seconds, a ding-dong of the bell
and an upward set of stairs later, and I was
banging on Jackson's bedroom door.

The thundering sound of shouty hip-hop
music instantly stopped, and a sheepish-
looking Jackson appeared.

'Oh, good – it's you!' Jackson sighed. 'I
thought it might be Mum!'

'Yeah? Well, it *could've* been your mum
and she *could've* caught you with Thing!'
I pointed out, hurrying into his room and
shutting the door firmly behind me.

'How did you know it was here?' Jackson
asked, puzzled.

What a donut.

'Well,' I answered, 'there's this amazing invention called a *window*, and guess what? You can see right through it!! Now where's Thing? I saw you giving it the Bucking Bronco treatment and it didn't look very happy . . .'

'It's fine! And it's in here . . .' said Jackson, pointing to his round, metal bin.

'But what's it doing inside in the first place?' I asked as I crouched down.

'Aw, Ruby, it was even *more* fed up than yesterday, cos of all the rain. And its friend the woodlouse doesn't say much. It just sits on that yellow jelly baby, when it's not scuttling off somewhere . . .'

As Jackson chattered, I peered into the bin and saw Thing, crumpled up in the bottom of it like an unwanted ball of furry paper.

'Are you OK?' I asked, reaching down to gently lift it out.

'No, *thank* you,' Thing purred ever so politely. 'Bumping-ing make me feel . . .'

I thought Thing was silent for a second because it was trying to remember the human word for 'sick'.

Unfortunately, it had stopped in the middle of its sentence because it was going to *be* sick.

'Urgh! Tissue, quick!' I ordered Jackson.

Boys, of course, don't tend to have useful things in their rooms like boxes of tissues (they have collections of empty DSi game boxes and odd socks instead).

By the time Jackson came back from the bathroom with a straggle of loo roll long

enough to wrap a real dead mummy in,
I'd already cleaned up Thing with a tissue
I'd found in my pocket and was giving it a
cuddle.

Oh, *and* telling it all about the school trip
and the Muir Wood exhibition just to take its
mind off barfing.

'. . . so after school on Friday, we'll be able
to come and tell you all about it!'

Thing blinked up at me, hanging on to
my every word.

It rubbed its paws together in circles.

Uh-oh.

I hadn't just taken its mind off barfing . . .
I'd got it all excited.

'I *like* to go to moo-zeem building-ing!' it
purred. 'I *like* to see wood again!'

'And don't forget, there's a genuine dead
Egyptian mummy and Viking horned
helmets!' Jackson blurted out.

'I *like* to see deaded mummy and horny-melts too, Rubby!' said Thing, rocking from side to side on my lap.

'No!' I said firmly to them both, hoping I sounded as stern as Miss Wilson, when she's in a particularly stern mood.

They both stopped smiling. Thing looked like it might cry.

'Why not?' asked Jackson.

WHY NOT?

Well, how about the fact that any time

Thing left the safety of the trees, crazy stuff happened.

Didn't either of them remember the house filled with butterflies?

Or the giant dancing noodles in the school dinner hall?

And don't get me started on the lilo that turned into the Loch Ness Monster at Ali's swimming party . . .

'Rubby?' Thing suddenly interrupted my thoughts. 'I *tell* you something?'

'Uh, OK,' I said warily.

It got up on to its tiptoes and gazed earnestly into my eyes. It was getting ready to beg to come on the school trip, I was sure. To tell me it would behave and promise not to do any magic. Just like it always did. (And then forgot.)

'Someone *coming*, Rubby!'

EEEK!

Thing was right! I could make out telltale creaks on the stairs outside!

'Jackson – turn the music back on!'

Five seconds later, Jackson's mum popped her head around the door.

'Good to see you're back to normal after your accident, Ruby!' she yelled above the sounds of the shouty hip-hop music.

Ha!

I was doing a one-eyed pogo around the room to a song I didn't like while hoping Mrs Miller didn't spot the weird squirrel/fairy/troll thing in the bin.

Right now, my life felt just about the OPPOSITE of normal.

And I also had a funny feeling that the trip to the museum wasn't going to end up being too normal either.

(Hate to spoil the story for you, but I was right, oh so right . . .)

Yum, yum, oops . . .

The next day, the sun was shining.

Only joking!

It was pouring with rain, heavier than ever . . .

The downpour had made school particularly annoying.

For the third day running, we'd had to stay in at break-time and lunch, which meant a whole classroom of fidgety kids getting more and more fidgety.

The boys in particular were going bananas (no surprise).

Jackson and Ali *said* they were all re-enacting Viking battles, but they just seemed to be roaring and crashing about like over-excited heffalumps.

They were acting so crazy that Mrs Nolan – the teaching assistant who was keeping an eye on us – had to go and drag Miss Wilson away from her sandwich in the staff room.

'It is TWO DAYS till the school trip!' she'd stomped in and bellowed in her *absolute* sternest voice. 'I want to see PERFECT BEHAVIOUR till then, or the trip is OFF!'

That scared the boys. They spent the rest of the lunch hour being good as gold, quietly drawing gruesome Viking battle scenes . . .

'So you see, we might not even be *going* to the museum!' I told Thing a few hours later, while spreading a plastic bag on a damp root knobble, so I could sit down.

(Me and my punctured eye were glad to see that Jackson had left his deadly umbrella at home, and was just wearing a cagoule.)

'Yeah, but then again, we still *might*!' Jackson added, unhelpfully.

Humph. Couldn't he see I was trying to let Thing down gently?

Of *course* it wanted to see photos of its old home.

But of *course* there was no *way* we were going to smuggle it on the school trip.

'Look, there'll be a guide book for sale, I'm sure,' I told Thing, who was huddled in the doorway of its home, the woodlouse sitting perched on the slightly stale yellow jelly baby beside it. 'I'll take my pocket money and buy one, so I can show you pictures afterwards.'

'Yes, *please*, Rubby,' Thing said sweetly. 'Um . . . what is guide hook?'

'Something boring that people buy and never look at,' Jackson yawned. 'Jelly baby?'

While Jackson and Thing stuffed their little and large faces, I decided to change the subject. (*Not* talking about the school trip and the museum seemed like a good idea.)

'So, I guess you can speak woodlouse, too?' I asked Thing.

Thing nodded. It was too polite to eat with its mouth open.

Jackson wasn't.

'G'won then!' he mumbled with his teeth jellified together. 'Tell's what a woodlouse speaks about!'

He pointed at the yellow jelly baby by Thing's side. The woodlouse wasn't so much eating it, as scuttling busily all over it.

'It talking to itself right *now*,' Thing purred. 'It say, 'Up . . .' then it say, '*Down* . . .' then it say, 'Up . . .' then it say, '*Down* . . .' then it say . . .'

'You know, I was just thinking, Ruby,'

Jackson completely and rudely interrupted Thing. (Though I was quite relieved. The woodlouse's conversation didn't sound too thrilling.)

'Oh, yeah?' I said, narrowing my eyes at him.

Jackson and thinking went together like ice cream and mince.

'I just don't think it's fair for Thing to miss this exhibition,' he said, offering round his bag of sweets. 'Not when it lived for like years in those woods.'

'Years and years and years,' mumbled

Thing, taking a green jelly baby. 'Years and years and years and years and *years* . . .'

For a split second, I wondered how many years that all added up to.

But I had no time for wondering.

I needed to get Jackson and Thing to understand that fair or not, **THING WAS DEFINITELY STAYING HOME ON FRIDAY.**

'Yeah, but—' Jackson tried to protest.

'No!' I replied.

'But we could—'

'No!'

'What if—'

'No!'

'Couldn't we just—'

'No!'

Thing's eyes ping-ponged back and forth between us, all the while silently chewing on its latest jelly baby.

And me and Jackson might have carried on with our bite-size argument all the way till our parents called us in for tea, if Thing hadn't made us jump out of our nylon jackets with shock.

'**EEEEEEEEEEEEEEK**!'

We froze – and stared at Thing.

Thing was staring at *us*, its eyes wider than wide – and brimming with tears . . .

In one of its paws was a pair of yellow jelly-baby feet.

And by its side, where once there had been a *whole* yellow jelly baby and a scuttling bug, was now *just an empty space*.

Gulp.

Thing had been distracted by us, and must've just reached out without thinking and, well, yum, yum, *oops* . . .

'Wow . . . did you just eat your *friend*?' Jackson asked bluntly.

A stunned Thing sat frozen to the spot, shaking ever so slightly.

Ping!

A tiny sparkle lit up the air behind one of
its ears.

Fizz!

There was another one, by the fern leaf under its feet.

'NO! *STOP*!!' I ordered Thing, realising that magic was just a crackle away.

To the left, over the wall and the fence, were our houses, mine and Jackson's.

To our right, through the trees, were the houses on Willow Avenue.

On a dull, drizzly day like today, *anyone* might spot cartwheels of sparkles – never mind whatever came next!

I reached out and scooped up our fretting friend.

'Eating the woodlouse was an accident, Thing!' I said quickly, giving it a comforting cuddle. 'Just an accident!'

Oh please, oh please, oh please, I whispered to myself. *Please let the magic NOT HAPPEN!*

'Hey . . .' I heard Jackson say, after a second or two. 'Nothing happened!'

I opened my eye and gazed around.
Sure enough, everything looked the same.
The trees were still trees, and we hadn't
been turned into slugs or any other random
strangeness.

What had gone so right?

'Thing? Thing? Did you manage to make
the magic stop?' I asked it in surprise.

But poor Thing was snivelling so much it
couldn't answer.

'Maybe crying dissolved the spell before it
started?' I suggested to Jackson, as I stroked
Thing's tear-soaked fur.

'Dunno,' Jackson replied uselessly. 'But
you know what *I* think? I think we've *got* to
cheer Thing up!'

'OK, but how?' I asked.

'Easy!' Jackson grinned. 'We let it come on
the school trip!!'

'Oooh!' cooed Thing, with a watery, small

smile. 'Yes, **PLEASE**, boy!'

Pah.

Thing might have been devastated at eating his buddy.

But maybe if I ate Jackson, it would be for the best . . .

Stopping the sparkles

It was Thursday afternoon, and me and Jackson were being mean to Thing.

We also planned to tease it.

We wanted to get it annoyed.

We were going to do our very best to get it all worrisome and flustery.

Don't panic; we were doing a proper scientific experiment. Sort of.

After yesterday – when Thing ate its

friend – I'd been pretty excited by the spell that had stopped before it had started.

'OK, maybe Thing *can* come on the school trip,' I'd said, as Jackson and Thing both looked at me with begging, puppy-dog eyes. 'But *only* if we test its AARGHH levels, and see if it can make the magic disappear again!'

They'd both agreed that was the best idea since jelly babies were invented.

So here we were – me, Jackson, Thing and a packet of Jammy Dodgers – all huddled inside my garden shed.

With the rain still endlessly raining, Mum had thought the shed was a great, fun place for me and Jackson to have as a den. ('Just don't poke each other with the garden shears,' she'd joked, while handing me the biscuits, as well as a few mushrooms. 'We don't need *another* trip to the hospital!')

What Mum *didn't* know was that the garden shed was a great place to test magic powers. With a bin bag taped across the window, no one would be able to see any stray sparkles of spells, if they happened to leak from Thing.

'What happen *now*, Rubby?' Thing

asked, wobbling anxiously on top of the workbench.

'Shut up!' Jackson barked at it.

Thing jumped, alarmed, but didn't start trembling, mainly because a big baboon grin had just broken out across Jackson's face.

'Jackson!' I said. '*Don't* laugh!!'

I mean, I was squirming in my Hawaiian floral camping chair too. Being horrible to Thing just didn't feel good, but we *had* to do it.

'OK, OK,' Jackson nodded, trying to rearrange his face into something more serious. (He looked like he was chewing a wasp.)

While he was getting his features under control, I thought I'd better get our experiment going for real.

'You know . . . I quite *like* squirrels,' I began. 'They're cute.'

Thing froze.

It hated squirrels.

It hated being compared to a squirrel.

Hopefully it hated me saying that I liked squirrels.

'Yeah!' Jackson joined in. '*And* cool!'

'Peh!' Thing grumbled in disgust, its squirrelly ears twitching with irritation.

Good.

Thing would be feeling AARGHH in no time at all.

It would be great to spark off some magic with only a bit of teasing, and without being too mean.

I was just trying to think of what to say next when Jackson jumped up from the upturned bucket he was sitting on and did something very peculiar.

'Uh–huh, squirrels are *cool*!' he rapped, jabbing his hands in front of him.

Yeah, they RULE!
They're nobody's FOOL!
And they, um . . . don't go to SCHOOL!

Me and Thing stared at Jackson.

As he awkwardly sat back down, the plastic bucket made a squeetling farty noise, as if it was giving its opinion of his terrible attempts at hip-hop.

'Rubby, what boy *doing*?' a confused Thing turned and asked me.

'YEAH, THEY RULE!'

'Acting like a big donut!' I said sarcastically. 'Jackson, we're meant to be helping *Thing* here, not auditioning for the *X-Factor*!'

Before the rap, Thing's AARGHH levels had been about four-out-of-ten and rising.

After, they'd dropped back down to zero, I was sure.

'I just thought it'd be a bit of fun!' Jackson shrugged.

'But we're not here to have fun!' I bellowed.

'Oh, come on, Ruby! You *never* want to have fun! You're *always* saying stuff like "No, we *can't*" and "*Don't* do this or that!".'

'I do not!' I snapped.

Though I knew deep down I *did* say stuff like that a lot, but only around Jackson and Thing, and only because I was the only sensible one out of the three of us.

'Do *so!*' Jackson baited me.

'Do *not!*' I growled.

'Do *so!*'

'Do *not!*'

'Do *so*, do *so*, do *so* times a hundred!'

AARGHH! Jackson Miller was making me *so* mad I felt like thunking the camping chair over his head and clamping it shut.

In class, he couldn't stop himself from acting the clown, and now, when we had an important job to do, he was being a total twerp. If only—

'Ruby!' he interrupted my silent rant. 'Ruby!! LOOK!!'

I glanced where he was pointing, and instead of seeing red, I saw stars.

Thing! It was swaying and shuddering in that telltale way.

Me and Jackson sniping at each other . . . it had made Thing all worrisome and

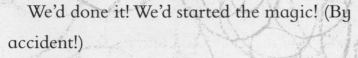

flustery!

We'd done it! We'd started the magic! (By accident!)

But now, could we stop it?

cRACKLE

'Thing!' I yelped. 'Try really hard not to let the magic out!'

'Not know *how*, Rubby!' Thing squeaked, as a fizz like a mini firework shot off across the flowerpots.

'Well . . . try concentrating! Say "STOP, STOP, STOP!" inside your mind! Close your eyes tight! Hold your breath!'

Wow. I don't know which of my burbled suggestions worked, but as the last hint of the mini-firework fizzled out, there was . . . nothing.

No crazy magic.

No flowerpots sprouting rainbow-coloured

golf umbrellas.

No Hawaiian floral camping chairs turning into horses and galloping off into the garden.

'Thing, you *did* it!' I laughed with relief.

'Yes, please?' purred Thing, rocking happily from side to side. 'I coming to moo-zeem now?'

'You are *so* coming on the school trip!' roared Jackson. 'Give me five!!'

Thing obviously didn't know what Jackson was on about (neither did I half the time).

But it very sweetly copied him and held up its tiny paw.

Which Jackson slapped hard, sending Thing flying off the top of the workbench with a thud and an 'Oof!' . . .

Extreme horribleness

'Hold on,' perhaps you're saying. 'Way, way back somewhere in this story, *you* said that the teeny-weeny woodlouse caused something big, bad and mad to happen.'

Yes, I did.

'But it got eaten a couple of chapters ago,' you might point out, 'so that can't be true, can it?'

Actually it IS true.

The woodlouse was just part of a chain of events.

What I mean is . . .

- If Thing hadn't made friends with the woodlouse, then it wouldn't have asked Jackson to give it a jelly baby.

- If the woodlouse hadn't liked scuttling on the jelly baby, Thing wouldn't have accidentally had it as a snack.

- If Thing hadn't got upset at eating it, we wouldn't have found out that Thing could sometimes, SOMEHOW control the magic.

- If Thing hadn't stopped the spell in mid-sparkle in the shed yesterday, then we wouldn't have risked letting it come on the school trip today.

Now do you get it?

'Um, I think so,' you might say warily. 'But when does the big, bad and mad stuff happen?'

Any minute now, trust me . . .

'Right! I'm going to pass these out to each of you,' said Miss Wilson, holding up some worksheets. 'There are questions to answer about what you see in each room, plus a sticker section to complete.'

The whole class was jiggling and shuffling in the entrance hall of the museum, keen to get going and explore.

Only me and Jackson were standing totally still.

Me, cos I was a little tense, and Jackson, cos he knew too much jiggling and shuffling might make Thing travel sick.

'Remember, we are not the *only* school visiting the museum today,' Miss Wilson announced. 'But I'd like to think that the other teachers here will be *wonderfully* impressed by your behaviour. Understand?'

'Yes, Miss Wilson!' we all bellowed, making the lady at the ticket desk jump.

With a rustle and a flutter of worksheets, everyone scampered off to different sections of the building.

Everyone except me and Jackson. We practically *glided* away, like swans in school uniform.

'Well done, Jackson,' said Miss Wilson with a nod. 'I'm liking what I'm seeing today!'

She didn't realise she was seeing a boy desperately trying not to jiggle the secret creature in his bag too much.

'Thank you, Miss Wilson,' said Jackson, his arms tucked protectively under the bottom of his back-to-front rucksack.

With him wearing it that way, Thing could see straight ahead, through the mesh panel under the clip fastener.

'So we're going to the Muir Wood exhibit first, right?' I said, looking around for directions.

'Yes, *please*, Rubby,' came a small voice.

'Shhh!' I whispered.

'Is it the Muir Wood exhibition you're after?' a voice suddenly asked, and I turned to see a smiley old man, wearing not a lot of hair on his head and a badge that said 'Museum Guide'.

'Um, yes!' I said brightly, hoping he hadn't heard me shushing the bag.

'Righto,' the Old Museum Guide nodded. 'Well, it's an audio-visual show, and it's through that door over th—'

'*RRRRAAAAA! HA! HA! HA!*' came a

sudden roar of laughter out of nowhere.

THUMP-WHACK!!

Two rushing, running boys crashed into me, Jackson and the Old Museum Guide, sending us all flying into a display of Iron Age arrow heads.

Saying sorry might have been nice.

Instead the boys looked at us, looked at each

other, then made a noise a little like this . . .

PFFFFFFFFFTTTTT!

It wasn't a nice noise. It was the sort of snigger people do when they see someone skateboarding into a bollard and breaking a shin or two.

Then they disappeared into the Ancient Civilisation section in a blur of red polo shirts with the OMG bumbling after them, ordering them NOT TO RUN.

They kept running.

'Idiots,' muttered Jackson.

'Peh,' muttered the bag.

'Forget about them. And let's go into the woods,' I said, while I straightened my dislodged eye padding.

Wow . . .

It really *was* a little like stepping into the woods.

Well, as much as an empty, darkened room

can look like woods.

Me and Jackson edged along
the back row of chairs, and sat
ourselves down, with the black
rucksack in between us.

'. . . *and of course the eco system
in the ancient woodland . . .*' a taped
voice boomed along to the giant
images of trees being flashed up
on the screen.

'Looks like everyone *else* is off

trying to find the dead mummies and the horned Viking helmets,' muttered Jackson, staring at the empty rows of seats in front of us, and getting out a rustly bag of jelly babies.

'Hey, any chance of you shutting up so we can watch this film?' I said, my one good eye glued to the screen.

'Yeah, whatever,' Jackson shrugged me off. 'But as there's no one here, we *could* let Thing out!'

'Well, I'm not sure—' I began, then stopped, when I saw that Thing was *already* sitting on Jackson's lap.

It was happily chewing on a jelly baby and picking at the sheet of stickers Miss Wilson had handed out.

'What *this* is, Rubby?' it mumbled, its eyes more saucer-shaped than ever in the semi-darkness.

'See the pictures on the stickers?' Jackson interrupted with an explanation. 'Like the Viking long ship here, and the arrow heads there? When we find the *real thing* in the museum, we put the matching sticker on our worksheet ...'

I reached across and pressed down two stickers that Thing was picking at. One was of a black outlined Egyptian eye. The other was a leaf, which I guessed represented what we were watching now.

Or were *supposed* to be watching.

'Look!' I said, pointing to the screen
and taking the sticker sheet out of Thing's
inquisitive paws. 'Do you recognise that tree?'

'... *was estimated to have grown from a
seed two hundred years ago ...*' boomed the
commentary, as a giant, gnarly old oak
flashed up, with sagging, twisty branches.

'Yes, it *good* tree,' Thing purred matter-of-
factly. 'But got too busy when big. Lots of

too many things live in it. I like it when it smaller. Quieter. *Mmm.'*

Er . . . Thing liked the oak when it was *smaller*? How *much* smaller? Ten years smaller? Forty years smaller? *More?!*

Before this, me and Jackson had been a little bit curious to know how old Thing was.

But *now* trying to work it out seemed pretty exciting, like solving a puzzle, maybe.

Still, it was hard to concentrate on films and furry puzzles when you were with Thing and Jackson.

'Boy! *When* you show me real dead mummy and horny-melt?' Thing suddenly babbled, turning to look up at Jackson. 'I like to see. What is horny-melt, boy?'

Huh? I didn't get this . . . Why did Thing seem so uninterested in the film, and Muir Wood?

'It's a *horned helmet*!' Jackson corrected it.

'Y'see, the Vikings got cows horns and superglued them on to their hats and—'

'What is *cow*, please?' Thing butted in sweetly.

'What's a *cow*?' gasped Jackson 'You *must* have seen one in the fields around the forest! They're big and go *mooooo*!!'

'*Moooo!*' purred Thing.

'HOLD IT!' I yelped. 'Thing, this film is about your *old home*! Aren't you at all interested?'

I waved my hand in the direction of the screen, where birds and bugs were scampering around amongst leafiness, ferns and fungus.

Thing blinked up at me, ladybirds reflected in its two moon eyes.

'But it just photies moving on wall, Rubby. It not *real*,' it said. 'I not get to *touch* it, or *smell* it. It no good. Peh.'

Hmm. I guess to humans, films can be amazing.

But maybe for a small, wild thing, it was like trying to lick a drawing of an ice lolly on a hot day (i.e. useless).

'*. . . of course, Mother Nature CAN play tricks, as it did in 1924, when a freak shower of snow blanketed Muir Wood in May . . .*'

Hold it!

A freak shower of snow in May?

Was that 'when sunny turn frosty'?

I mean, the time when Thing said his old woodlouse friends died?

It couldn't have happened *that* long ago!

Could it?

Could it?!

'Right, let's go and look at something else,' Jackson announced, while my brain felt as scrambled as an egg.

But before either of us could say or do anything else, the door thunked open.

FLAP-A-DAP-A-DAP!

Two figures burst into the room.

The beam of back-light streaming in from the corridor showed they were wearing red

polo shirts.

'Thing, *hide!*' I whispered.

Under my arm, I could feel the squiggle of Thing nuzzling back down into its hidey-hole bag.

'BOR-*INNGG!*' one of the figures called out.

'Hey, race you!' yelped the other, and leapt on to a chair, running the whole length of a row – seat by seat.

FLAP-A-DAP-A-DAP!

Another figure lumbered in, flipping on the lights, leaving me and Jackson blinking madly.

'You two! Off those chairs *now*!' barked the OMG, at the boys.

'No problem, Grandad!' one of them laughed, pushing right past him, while tapping the OMG on the top of his bald head.

The boy's mate sniggered, and they both loped out into the corridor.

How awful were they?

So awful that they made Jackson seem sweet as a fairy princess . . .

I just hoped Thing wasn't too freaked out by these trouble twins and their extreme horrible-ness.

Gently, I gave the rucksack a reassuring pat.

But the rucksack went completely *flat*.

Eeek!

'It's gone!' I squeaked.

'What?' said Jackson, with a jelly-baby-sized bump in his cheek.

'What?' said the OMG, with a sticker of a leaf now attached to his shiny forehead.

Those boys . . . they thought stickering an innocent old man was funny, did they?

Well, they were just about to find out that it WASN'T funny to mess with a small, freaked-out furball called Thing.

Or its friends.

A missing Thing

We looked for Thing in the Roman section.

No luck.

The Iron Age section.

Nothing.

The Medieval period.

Zilch.

'How will we be able to find it amongst all these people?' I panicked, as we weaved through a bunch of kids in red polo shirts.

Just then, a clue wafted past my ears.

'It was *so* cute!' a kid from the other

school was saying to her friend. 'No *way* did it look a zillion years old, like from proper Egyptian times and everything!'

'I *know*!' said her classmate. 'It seemed practically *alive*!'

I shot a glance at Jackson.

We both knew who . . .

looked cute, and

was most definitely alive.

'This way!' Jackson called out to me, dragging me by my cardie in the direction of a grand doorway with two giant stone falcons sitting on either side.

Hmm.

One of those stone falcons had an empty packet of cheese and onion crisps wedged over its beak.

For about a millisecond,
I wondered who might do
something yucky like that, and then
I knew for sure.

Over by a roped-off display were
two boys.

In matching red polo shirts.

The Trouble Twins.

'Man, that thing is *well* weird!' one of
them was saying.

'Look, Ruby! Over *there*!' Jackson
hissed.

Thing!

It was standing statue-still
on a long, high platform
surrounded by odd bumpy,
bandaged shapes.

Wait a minute — I remembered this
display from the *last* time I visited the

museum, when I was about eight.

Me and Dad had stood looking at the bandaged bumps, reading about how Egyptians didn't just mummify their pharaohs; they bundled up their *pets* too . . .

'It says here,' muttered the other Trouble Twin, moving his finger along the description plaque, 'that these are cats, fish, birds and snakes. The big one's a baboon. So what's *that* supposed to be?'

Even from behind, we could see he was nodding at Thing.

'Dunno, but let's check it out!' sniggered

Trouble Twin 1.

He glanced either side, and saw that everyone in the room had their backs to him.

Everyone except us – he hadn't spotted me and Jackson, sneaking up behind.

Thinking he was safe, the boy leaned *right* across the large, red-lettered 'Do Not Touch!' sign and made a lunge.

Bet you can guess what he was lunging for . . .

'Don't you dare!' I hissed, hurrying over and grabbing him by the arm.

'Gerroff!' Trouble Twin 1 growled, wriggling away from me and bounding up on to the platform.

'You can't!' I yelped.

'You want a bet?' he said cheerfully, as he grabbed Thing and tucked it under his arm.

'Hey, pirate girl!' Trouble Twin 2 suddenly distracted me. 'See any better *now*?'

With that, he gave my patched eye a pat
with his hand.

'Ha, ha, ha!' he sniggered, for no apparent
reason.

'Oi!' said Jackson. 'What d'you think
you're doing?'

But Trouble Twin 2 wasn't listening – he
was too busy having Thing passed like a
parcel to him, while his idiot friend made
a grab for something else before roaring
'RUN!!!'. . .

Without stopping to think, me and
Jackson ran after them too, dodging in
and out of meandering school groups and
teachers.

'*I* see them!' Jackson said. 'Follow me!'

I followed, hurtling through a swing door
and straight into a tiled room.

We were in the loos.

The *men's* loos.

(I'd have been totally embarrassed, if I hadn't been busy being stressed.)

Over by the sinks were the Trouble Twins, about to examine their stolen treasure.

I expected them to look up at me and Jackson as soon as we barged in ... but they were too wrapped up in staring at Thing.

'Jay! *Jay*, man!' I heard Trouble Twin 1 blurt out to his buddy. 'It's ... it's *staring* at me! And ... and it's *moving*!'

Thing was doing *more* than just moving.

It was trembling.

Oh, no ... we couldn't have spells happening here!

After all, this was a museum, heaving with people. Which meant *anyone* could walk into the toilets and see whatever spell was coming next.

Thing would get spotted.

Thing would be in trouble!

This was BIG.

(I had no idea right then that it was about to get BAD and MAD too, of course.)

'Don't!' I called out. 'STOP THE MAGIC!'

Thing glanced over at me.

Uh-oh.

I'd meant to remind Thing that it could stop the crackles and sparkles from starting, if it really, really tried.

But instead, it must've just heard the sentence as 'Don't stop the magic!'

Cos all of a sudden there was a . . .

CRACKLE
SPIT
FIZZZZzZZ!!

Flickers of light danced across the shiny tiles on the walls, as if someone had set off a sparkler.

The sparkles glittered and cartwheeled around the loos, bouncing off the mirrors, the walls and the sinks.

But then – just as soon as the mini-fireworks show started – it *stopped*.

There was a second of silence and held breaths. Then . . .

'*Moooooo!*'

Mooooo? That couldn't be good. Strange moooooing in a public toilet HAD to be BAD.

'Sam! SAM!' screeched the boy called Jay, holding up a bundle of bandages that I recognised as the baboon from the dead Egyptian animal display. He must have swiped *that*, after he'd passed Thing to his mate!

'*Moooooo!*' said the bandaged baboon.

Huh? Why was this mummified monkey
moo-ing? Then I realised . . . Jackson had
been making that sound not long ago.
Which must've left Thing with a head full of
cows!

'AARGHH!!' screamed both the boys.

'*Moooooo!*' mooed the baboon.

With a thud, Jay dropped the mummy to

the ground, kicking it away hard.

'Moooooo!'

With an underarm throw, Sam hurled
Thing as far away from him as he could.

'Eek!' it squeaked, sailing through the air.

Jackson made a dive that our PE teacher
would have been proud of, neatly catching
Thing in his arms with a shower of new
sparkles.

New sparkles = new magic.

Help!

What *now*?

SHUMF! SHUMFF-
SHUMFF-
SHUMFF!

SHUMF! SHUMFF-SHUMFF-SHUMFF!
SHUMFF!

The baboon mummy lay still and silent on the floor, the first spell undone.

The Trouble Twins stood silent and shocked by the far wall.

Actually, they were standing in the strangest way . . . their red polo shirts and grey shorts pulled out at sharp, pointy angles.

'Let us down!' the one called Sam shrieked.

'We're sorry!!' yelped the one called Jay.

'They're stuck to the wall!' gasped Jackson. 'By arrow heads!'

The Iron Age flint arrow heads . . . from the case we'd stumbled into earlier, me, Jackson and the Old Museum Guide.

The *SHUMF! SHUMFF-SHUMFF-SHUMFF*ing had been the sound of them whizzing through the air and pinning the

boys to the wall by their clothes.

Oooh, this was getting seriously MAD.

'Rubby?' purred Thing.

'Yes, Thing?' I answered, staring dumbly at the Trouble Twins.

'Somebody *coming*, Rubby!'

AARGHH!

Footsteps!

Thundering footsteps just outside!

'In *there*,' I said, shoving Jackson and Thing into the nearest cubicle.

I closed the door – and realised we were in a cleaner's cupboard. Which was the safest place to be, it turned out, even if I *did* have a mop handle poking me in the back.

THWACK! We heard the door into the loos burst open.

'SAM! JAY! What on EARTH have you two been up to?' came the sound of a man's voice.

A stern, teacherly voice, I was sure.

'Like I say, they've been up to all sorts!' came a breathless, older man's voice. 'I've been chasing 'em around the museum all this time, trying to stop them!'

'Help us, Mr Smith!' called out one of the boys. 'We've been shot at by arrows!'

'They must've stole those out of a cabinet!'
gasped the OMG. 'Thousands of years old,
they are! Priceless!'

'But we *didn't*!' protested another boy's
voice. 'We only took the baboon mummy
and that . . . that *thing*!'

'Yeah – and the boy and the girl who are
in here. *They* saw! *They* must have shot the
arrows!'

I felt Jackson flinch beside me in the dark.

'Really?' said the disbelieving voice of

the male teacher. 'And where might this arrow-firing boy and girl be? In one of these cubicles, perhaps?'

WHOOSH-thud.

WHOOSH-thud.

WHOOSH-thud.

WHOOSH-thud.

Four cubicle doors were flung open.

The cleaner's cupboard door stayed thankfully shut.

'No sign of your imaginary friends in *here*, boys,' their teacher positively growled. 'Now, this gentleman *WHOSE HEAD YOU STICKERED* will carefully remove these valuable artefacts. Then we are going *straight* back to school to see what the head teacher has to say about your behaviour!'

In the next couple of minutes, while the OMG unpinned them, the Trouble Twins whinged and 'But, Sir!'d a whole heap of times, but it didn't do them any good.

Finally, they were marched out, with a last, safe *THWACK* of the main door.

We were free.

'Thought I was going to sneeze, with that smell of disinfectant in there!' said Jackson, blinking in the light.

As he spoke, I saw his reflection in the mirror, and couldn't help let out a giggle.

It wasn't the sight of him stuffing Thing safely into his bag.

It was the fact that he was wearing a yellow duster on his head at a jaunty angle.

'Looking good yourself, Ruby!' grinned Jackson, pointing at *my* reflection.

Oh.

I had *two* eyes.

One normal one, and one Egyptian, black-rimmed one, stuck on my padding, thanks to the Trouble Twins . . .

'Hey, did you hear what Sam and Jay got caught doing?' said a voice, as a boy and his mate barged into the room.

'*Sneck!*' came a small noise from inside Jackson's rucksack.

The boys in red polo shirts stopped dead.

I don't know whether it was because they were shocked to walk into a men's toilets and come across . . .

a boy with a duster on his head,
a girl,
a girl with a weird stickered eye,
a sneezing bag, or
all four.

But what I *did* know was it was time to get out of there.

'Coming?' I said to Jackson, as casually as I could.

'Sneck!' sneezed the bag, as we wandered past two *very* confused-looking boys . . .

10

Older than a very old thing

It was Saturday morning and still raining.

Swoosh-swish, swoosh-swish went the windscreen wipers as Mum and me drove home from the supermarket.

'What *is* Jackson doing?' asked Mum, peering along our lane.

I stared too, using *both* my eyes. (After the museum trip yesterday, Dad had taken me to the hospital for a check-up, and I'd had my padded pirate patch taken off for good.)

'It looks as if he's *reading*!' I said in surprise.

It was surprising because Jackson only ever reads . . .

instructions for new computer games,
or

books that Miss Wilson **MAKES** him read.

Even more weird was the fact that Jackson was reading something under an umbrella and opposite my cottage.

'Hello, Mrs Morgan!' called Jackson, as soon as Mum parked the car and we got out.

'Hi, Jackson! What are you up to?' she called back, hurrying to grab bags of shopping out of the boot.

'Uh, y'know . . . just hanging out!' he answered her brightly.

'You and your friend,' Mum said to me under her breath. 'What is it with you two being out in all weathers?'

'I'll just see what's going on . . .' I mumbled back, throwing my hood up over my head.

'OK, but don't get *too* soaked, Ruby!' Mum said, as she hurried through the gate and up the path.

'I won't!' I told her, wondering why Jackson had such a fake, fixed smile on his face.

Was it to do with what he was holding?
Nope.

It was a booklet called *Memories of Muir Wood*. Jackson had bought a copy of it from the museum shop yesterday. We hid behind it as we watched Sam and Jay getting frogmarched out of the building by the Old Museum Guide.

But *then* I got what the fake smile was about…

'Ta-da!' sing-songed Jackson, as he lowered the booklet.

'Rubby!' Thing purred in delight, its little head peeking over the top of Jackson's zipped-up rain jacket.

'What are you two *doing* out here?' I demanded, as I dipped gingerly under the shelter of the dangerous umbrella.

'Well, we were a bit bored this morning, cos you'd gone off with your mum,' Jackson began. 'So first, we played a little dressing-up game . . .'

With the hand that *wasn't* holding the booklet, Jackson slid his zip down just low enough for me to see that Thing's whole tiny body appeared to be wrapped in toilet paper.

'Look! We play *real* dead mummies!' Thing purred happily. *'Mooo!'*

I narrowed my eyes at Jackson.

'So *after* you wrapped Thing in loo roll, you thought it'd be nice to take it for a stroll in the rain, and look at a guide book?' I suggested, thinking that Jackson's brain wasn't just extra, *extra* small. It had to be extra, extra, extra, extra, *extra* small, at *least*.

'Yeah, cause I wanted to show Thing a photo in here,' said Jackson, holding up *Memories of Muir Wood*.

'You mean, you actually *read* it?' I gasped.

I thought Jackson had only bought the book for cover.

Wow, I was quite impressed.

'Well, not *exactly*.' Jackson shrugged. 'When I got home, I tried to chuck it in the bin in my bedroom. But I missed, and it fell open at *this* page . . .'

I found myself looking at a black and white photo of my cottage.

The tall, wafty flowers looked much the same as they did now.

The cottage too.

The main difference was the thick forest you could see behind it (all gone now, except for the few sad, stray trees that got left behind).

And of course the lady in the long, old-fashioned frock by the gate.

No one dressed like *that* any more. Not

unless they were going to a fancy-dress party as Queen Victoria or someone.

'Guess what Thing just said about this picture?!' asked Jackson excitedly.

'I don't know. What did you say, Thing?'

Thing blinked at me.

'I say I seen ladies like that, Rubby. *Lots*. Ladies like that walkie-walkie through my woods. But not for long time. Not for long, long, long—'

'You mean you remember people *wearing* stuff like this?' I interrupted.

I stared at Thing, all swaddled up like a baby, and realised with a thump of shock that the photo must've been taken at *least* a hundred years ago! Which matched with Thing saying how it preferred the oak tree in the museum film when it was much smaller . . .

'And I see people wear wrappings same

as *this* too, Rubby,' Thing added, tapping a furry finger on a drawing below the photo. 'They come choppy-choppy trees, long, long, long time ago. Long, long, long, long, *long* time ago.'

Its big round eyes were fixed on an illustration of a bearded man in a leather hat, a long tunic and a cloak. He was carrying an axe.

'*Nearby Viking settlements resulted in swathes of Muir Wood being cut down, circa* AD *900*', the caption read.

'Jackson . . .' I muttered, going hot and cold and prickly and shivery all at the same time. 'Do you understand what this could mean?'

Thing, our lovely little Thing, was older than a very, *very* old thing indeed.

'Wow, yeah!' Jackson burst out. 'Of course! It means the dude who drew this got it *well* wrong — I mean, can you believe it? There are *no* horns on his helmet, and this guy's supposed to be a *Viking*!'

Sigh.

Jackson might not be mummified, but he certainly was a big baboon.

I did the only thing I could . . .

Reaching over with one hand, I scooped Thing, who gave a startled 'EEEK!', from inside Jackson's jacket.

Then with the other hand, I pressed the stud high up on the stem of the handle and let the umbrella collapse over my stupid friend's stupid head.

'Bye!' I said breezily, ducking under and walking away, while Jackson mumphfed and 'Oi'd!' behind me.

So, after all that, did we solve the mystery of *exactly* how old Thing is?

Er . . . no.

(Trying to figure out facts about Thing is as hard as juggling jelly.)

Thing is old for sure, though maybe not quite *Viking* old.

Yes, I know it seemed to recognise the drawing of the bearded man in the museum booklet.

But Thing *could've* made a mistake.

I mean, it's not just Vikings who have beards. My uncle has one, and he is definitely *not* a Viking, or I'm sure my auntie would've mentioned it.

But no matter how old Thing is (or isn't), me and Jackson *do* know we love our strange little friend.

And we know that Thing loves us.

It also loves the waterproof jacket Jackson made for it, for next time it rains.

'Is *nice*!' Thing says approvingly, as it

rustles inside the empty jelly-baby bag.

Phew.

Now it has its jelly-baby raincoat, *next* time the weather is bad, Thing won't get fed up, and won't go where it shouldn't go, and won't get into any trouble.

(And if you believe that, I'm a three-thousand-year-old Egyptian baboon . . . !)